LET'S HAVE A PARTY #4

SURPRISE!

Other Avon Camelot Books in the
LET'S HAVE A PARTY *Series by*
Laura E. Williams

#1: School's Out!
#2: Splash!
#3: Sleepover

Coming Soon

#5: Boo Who?

LET'S HAVE A PARTY #4

SURPRISE!

LAURA E. WILLIAMS

Illustrations by
George Ulrich

AVON BOOKS
A division of
The Hearst Corporation
1350 Avenue of the Americas
New York, New York 10019

Interior illustrations by George Ulrich
Published by arrangement with the author
Visit our website at **http://AvonBooks.com**
Library of Congress Catalog Card Number: 97-92888
ISBN: 0-380-78921-3
RL: 2.3

First Avon Camelot Printing: August 1997

Printed in the U.S.A.

OPM 10 9 8 7 6 5 4 3 2 1

This book is dedicated to
Madeline Stover Williams
and her wonderful parents—
with love

1

Left Out

Lucy Falwell hurried out of the classroom. She ran over to her friends standing next to the swings.

They stopped talking as she approached.

"Miss W made me finish copying my spelling words," Lucy said. "What are you talking about?"

Her friends glanced at each other.

"Nothing," Tasha said with a smirk.

"But I saw you talking," Lucy insisted.

"No," Pegi said, pulling her baseball cap over her eyes. "We were just standing around. Let's go take the basketball away from the boys."

Lucy watched her friends run away from her. Why were they pretending they hadn't been talking before?

She *saw* them *talking*.

Molly stopped to tie her shoe.

Lucy walked over to her. "Do you want me to come over tomorrow? I can help you with your math like I always do."

Molly shook her head. "No thanks. I have to help my dad, uh, wash the cars."

"But that won't take all day," Lucy said.

Molly stood up. "My dad is very picky. We have to wash the cars inside and out."

"Hmmm," said Lucy. "Then how about on Sunday?"

Molly rubbed her chin. "Noooo," she said slowly. "I have to . . . I have to . . ."

"You have to what?" Lucy asked.

"Oh, I remember. I have to help my mom wash the cars."

Lucy crossed her arms and tapped her foot.

"But you said you were doing that on Saturday. With your *dad*."

Molly nodded. "Yup, but my mom is even pickier than my dad. I have to do it again on Sunday. With my *mom*."

Lucy narrowed her eyes. Something sounded awfully suspicious. But Molly ran off to the see-saws before she could question her more.

"Hey, Pegi," Lucy called. She ran over to her friend. "Do you want to come over this weekend?"

Pegi bounced the basketball. "I can't."

"Why not?"

"Uh, I have to help my five brothers clean the house," Pegi said.

Timmy grabbed the ball away from Pegi. Pegi raced after him.

Lucy looked around. Lesley and Maryellen were whispering and giggling by the water fountain. She ran over to them.

"Hi," Lesley said.

"Hi," Maryellen said.

Lucy smiled. At least these two friends weren't ignoring her. "Do you want to come over this weekend?" she asked them. "I could show you how I made those dresses for my dolls."

Lesley and Maryellen looked at their shoes.

"I have to clean my horse's stall this weekend," Lesley said.

"That's right," Maryellen said quickly. "And I have to clean my cat's litter box."

"But you don't even have a cat," Lucy protested.

Maryellen's face turned red. "I know. But I'm going to maybe get one this weekend."

Lucy's shoulders drooped. "So you'll both be busy all weekend?"

The two girls nodded.

Just then, the bell rang. Recess was over.

Lucy shuffled into school with her shoulders sagging. Her friends ran in ahead of her.

Why did it seem as if no one liked her anymore? They weren't exactly being mean, but they *were* acting strange.

Lucy shook her head. Maybe she was just imagining it. After school everything would be back to normal.

2

After School

After school, Lucy waited by the front doors for her friends.

She waited.

And waited.

And waited.

Dr. Petersen walked by. "Lucy, what are you doing here? School is over."

Lucy looked up at the principal. He had a

bald head. She and the kids at school called him melon head when he wasn't around.

"I know," Lucy said. "I'm waiting for Tasha and Maryellen. We always walk home together."

The principal raised his bushy eyebrows. "I don't think there are any more children here."

"But we always wait for each other," Lucy said. "They wouldn't leave without me."

"Then let's go check the rooms," Dr. Petersen said.

Lucy followed the principal down the hall. They checked room 107. Empty.

Room 108. Empty.

Room 109. Empty.

"I think they're all gone," said the principal.

Lucy blinked back her tears. "But we always wait for each other."

Dr. Petersen took her hand. He led her back to the office. "They probably just forgot. Let me call your mother to tell her you'll be late."

Lucy sat on the bench in the office. Her heart felt very heavy. It had sunk down to her stomach.

She sighed.

She wasn't imagining it.

DR. PETERSON
PRINCIPAL

Third grade was supposed to be fun. But here it was, just the start of the year, and for some reason no one liked her. If only she knew what she had done wrong. Then she could make it right again. Then they would be her friends again.

Dr. Petersen came out of his office and said, "Your mother wants you to come right home. She said you could walk alone." He gave her a big smile.

Lucy nodded and tried to smile back. "It's only one block."

"Have a wonderful weekend," Dr. Petersen called after her.

Lucy only waved. She knew it would be a horrible weekend. But at least Dr. Petersen was nice. She would never call him melon head again.

When she got home, she slammed the kitchen door behind her. "Where's Maddy?" she asked her mother.

"Your sister is at dance class."

Lucy sighed. She dropped her school bag next to the kitchen table.

"What's the matter?" her mother asked.

"Nothing," Lucy said.

"Nothing?" Mrs. Falwell put down her pencil and calculator and hugged Lucy. "I think something is bothering you."

"I don't feel good," Lucy said. "Maybe I have a terrible sickness."

Her mother felt Lucy's forehead. "I don't feel a fever. Open your mouth."

Lucy opened her mouth.

"Say ah," said Mrs. Falwell.

"Ahhhhh."

"I don't see anything wrong," she said, standing up. "How was school?"

Lucy watched her mother pour two glasses of milk. "I missed half of recess. I had to finish copying my spelling words off the board."

Mrs. Falwell handed Lucy a glass of milk and a banana. "Is that why you're sad?"

"I guess so," Lucy said. She bit into the banana.

Mrs. Falwell sat down with her glass of milk. "Let me tell you a secret," she said. Lucy's mother leaned forward and whispered, "This is what I do when I have the blues."

"The blues?" asked Lucy. "What are the blues?"

3
The Blues

"That's what people say when they're sad," explained Mrs. Falwell.

"What do you do?"

Mrs. Falwell wiggled her eyebrows. "I take a bath."

Lucy swallowed a mouthful of milk. "A bath?"

"A bubble bath!" Mrs. Falwell said. "It washes away the blues."

"Oh," Lucy said, finishing her banana. She didn't see how a bubble bath would wash away the blues. Maybe it would wash away blue paint. Or blue ink. But not a blue feeling.

Her mother wiped away her milk mustache. "Do you want to try it?"

"A bath before dinner?"

Mrs. Falwell stood up. "Sure! Why not? There's no wrong time for a bath. Come on."

Lucy followed her mother up to the bathtub.

Mrs. Falwell turned on the water. Then she took a pink bottle out of the cabinet. "This is the secret ingredient."

Lucy sat down and pulled off her shoes and socks. "What is it?"

"It's bubble bath." Mrs. Falwell poured some into the tub. "It's called Pink Perfection. And it's guaranteed to wash away the blues."

Bubbles frothed under the gushing water faucet. Lucy watched in amazement as bubbles grew and grew. They smelled sweet.

Her mother turned off the water. "In you go," she said. "Just sit back and close your eyes. And your blues will wash down the drain when you get out."

Lucy climbed into the water. She sat down.

The bubbles rose up around her. They tickled her nose.

"I'll be back in a little while," said Mrs. Falwell.

Lucy nodded. She tried to push some of the bubbles out of the way, but they just kept coming back.

Finally she gave up. She leaned back against the edge of the tub. The hot water did feel good. If only there weren't so many bubbles.

She tried not to think about her friends, but she couldn't help it. Her heart still felt heavy. All the light, fluffy bubbles around her didn't help.

Mrs. Falwell came back a little while later. "How do you feel?"

Lucy lifted a hand and looked at it. "Like a prune. And I look like one, too."

"Oh dear," Mrs. Falwell said. She looked at the bubble bath bottle and shook her head. "Pink Perfection always works for me."

Lucy got out of the tub. She watched the water swirl down the drain. She sighed. Her blues were still with her. They hadn't washed down the drain after all.

Just then, Mr. Falwell and Maddy came home. "We're home," he called. "Hello?"

Mrs. Falwell went downstairs while Lucy got dressed. She put on her favorite rainbow shirt and some purple shorts. Rainbows and unicorns always cheered her up. Only they didn't seem to be working this time.

She was just brushing her hair when her father knocked on her door.

"Come in," she said.

Mr. Falwell came in and sat on the edge of her bed. "I hear you have the blues."

Lucy nodded.

He wiggled his finger like a worm. Lucy knew that meant to go to him. He hugged her.

"Let me tell you a secret," he said.

4

In the Dumps

"This is what I do when I'm in the dumps," Lucy's father said.

"In the dumps?" Lucy repeated.

Mr. Falwell nodded. "Sure. It means the same thing as having the blues."

"Oh," Lucy said. "What do you do?"

Her dad squeezed her tight. "I cook."

"Cook?"

"I cook up a storm. You've seen me do that. Sometimes I bake a cake. Or I make bread. Or I cook something special for your mom." Mr. Falwell took the brush from Lucy. He slowly brushed her hair. "Do you want to try it?"

Lucy shrugged. The bubble bath hadn't worked. But maybe cooking was just the thing. "Okay," she said.

Mr. Falwell put down the brush and swung Lucy around. "Yahoo," he shouted. "Let's go cook!"

In the kitchen, Lucy's dad pulled out the waffle maker. "We'll make waffles and have them for dinner."

Lucy's stomach growled. Good idea. She loved waffles.

Her dog stuck his big black nose in her side.

"Go away, Boo," she said, giggling. His nose tickled her.

The dog nudged her again.

She bent down and whispered, "I'll save one of the waffles for you."

Boo snorted.

"Go on," Lucy said. She waved her hands at him.

Boo sat down at her side.

"I said go on." Lucy tried to push the giant dog out of the way.

Boo wouldn't budge.

Finally Lucy gave up.

Mr. Falwell lay out the ingredients on the table. "First you measure three cups of flour into the bowl."

Lucy carefully measured one cup. She dumped it into the big yellow bowl.

She measured the second cup and dumped that into the bowl.

She measured the third cup. Carefully, she lifted it out of the flour container. Just then Boo tickled her leg with his nose.

Up went her hands. Up flew the flour.

Most of the flour landed right away. On the table. On the floor. On her dad. On Boo.

And some of the flour floated down slowly. It looked like snow.

"Oops," Lucy said.

Her dad sighed. Then he smiled. But he didn't look as cheery as he had a minute ago.

"Just a little spill," Mr. Falwell said. "We'll clean it up later." He handed her the eggs. "Be careful," he warned.

Lucy cracked the eggs and dropped them in

ALL PURPOSE
FLOUR

the bowl. No egg landed on the floor. A couple of shells did go in the bowl, though. Lucy quickly stirred them in.

Mr. Falwell measured in the other dry ingredients. "Now for the milk. Do you want me to do it?" he asked.

"I can do it," Lucy said. She took the milk and the measuring cup.

When she was done, her father said, "Perfect. Isn't cooking wonderful?"

Lucy looked at the mess on the floor. She nodded anyway.

Mr. Falwell handed her a wooden spoon. "Now just mix it all together."

Lucy took the spoon and wrapped an arm around the bowl. She started to mix. Milk sloshed up over the side.

"Careful," Mr. Falwell said. He had a funny look on his face. Like he'd just seen a skunk.

Lucy mixed until her dad told her to stop.

"Not bad," he said.

Lucy scowled. There was more batter on the table and on the floor than in the bowl.

Her father sighed. "I guess you'd better let me finish this. The waffle iron gets very hot."

Lucy nodded. So much for cooking to get her out of the dumps.

At least Boo was happy. He got to lick the batter off the floor.

5

Tea Party

"Time to eat," Mr. Falwell called.

Lucy sat down at the table. Maddy sat across from her.

"Mmmm, waffles," Maddy said. She licked her lips. "I love waffles."

Mrs. Falwell sat down. "Daddy and Lucy made them," she said. She cut up her waffle and poured syrup over the pieces. She took a bite. Crunch.

Mr. Falwell took a bite. Crackle.

Maddy took a bite. Crunch crackle. "Yuk," she said. "What's in these waffles?"

Lucy took a small bite. Crackle crackle crunch. She made a face. "Eggshells!"

Maddy pushed away her plate. "I want peanut butter and jelly. I won't eat any more eggshells."

They all had peanut butter and jelly sandwiches and tomato soup.

After dinner, Lucy fiddled with her fork.

"Aren't you going to call one of your friends?" Mrs. Falwell asked.

Lucy shook her head. "Not tonight."

Mrs. Falwell looked at Mr. Falwell.

Lucy wondered why her mother didn't say anything. Maybe she knew Lucy's friends didn't like her anymore.

Lucy stood up. "I guess I'll go to my room now."

Her parents nodded. Boo followed her upstairs.

In her room, Lucy sat on the floor. Boo sat next to her.

"What can I do to feel better?" Lucy said out loud. She looked around her room. "I can color." Then she frowned. "No, I'll just feel sadder if I go out of the lines. I can read." She sighed. "No, Tasha still has the book I was reading. And Tasha isn't my friend anymore. I don't have any friends."

Boo licked her face.

Lucy hugged Boo. "At least you're my friend."

Boo licked her again.

"I know," Lucy said, wiping away Boo's slobber. "We'll have a tea party. Tea parties always made me feel better when I was little."

Lucy arranged her small teapot and tiny teacups on a tray. She pretended to pour a cup for Boo, but it really wasn't tea. It was just air. Then she pretended to pour a cup for herself.

Boo nudged the tray with his nose. The tray flew up into the air.

"Oh no," Lucy cried. "You've ruined the tea party, Boo."

Boo barked.

"Okay, I'm sorry I yelled at you," she said. "I don't want to fight with the only friend I have left."

6

For Sale

The next morning, Lucy awoke with a wonderful idea. She ran downstairs.

Mr. Falwell was cooking in the kitchen.

Mrs. Falwell was working with her calculator at the kitchen table.

"Mom, Dad, we have to move!" Lucy said.

Mr. Falwell put down his wooden spoon. "What?"

Mrs. Falwell put down her pencil. "What?"

"We have to move to a new neighborhood," Lucy explained.

"Why?" asked Mr. Falwell.

Lucy leaned on the counter. "You're always complaining about all the stuff that needs fixing, Dad. The leaky roof, the groaning pipes, the wet basement. If we move, we can have a strong roof, quiet pipes, and a dry basement."

Lucy moved to the table and sat down. "And, Mom, you always wanted a bigger yard so you could have a garden."

"But I thought you liked this neighborhood," Mrs. Falwell said. "You're close to all your friends."

Lucy looked down at the table and didn't say anything.

Mr. Falwell coughed. "I think it would be very hard to sell this house, anyway. The housing market is very bad right now." He picked up his spoon and started stirring again.

"That's true," said Mrs. Falwell. "It took almost two years for our neighbors to sell their house." She picked up her pencil and started writing down numbers again.

Lucy ran up to her room. She didn't know what a housing market was. But she knew that if she could sell the house, they could move to a new neighborhood. And all her problems would be solved.

In her room, she got out her favorite markers. Next, she pulled a piece of cardboard out from under her bed. Very carefully, she made a sign.

When she was done, she stood back and looked at it.

"Perfect," she said. "Now someone will buy our house."

With her sign, Lucy ran downstairs and outside. The September sun burned down bright and hot.

Lucy sat cross-legged on the front yard. Boo lay down next to her and panted. She held her sign up. She wished she had a cool, shady tree in the front yard like the house next door did.

She counted the cars that drove by.

Each person who drove by waved and smiled at her. But no one stopped to buy the house.

Mrs. Higgins walked down the sidewalk with her dog. "Hello, Lucy. Hello, Boo."

Boo lifted his head.

Lucy smiled. "Hi, Mrs. Higgins."

"I see you're holding a FOR SALE sign," said Mrs. Higgins.

FOR SALE

Lucy nodded.

"It's a beautiful sign." Higgy, Mrs. Higgins's dog, yipped and pulled on the leash. "Even Higgy likes it," Mrs. Higgins said, smiling. "Tell me, how much do you cost?"

"How much do *I* cost?" Lucy said. "But *I'm* not for sale, the *house* is."

"Oh, I thought *you* were for sale. Silly me!" Mrs. Higgins threw back her head and laughed.

Higgy yipped and yapped. Boo barked.

When she finally stopped laughing, Mrs. Higgins wiped her eyes and said, "Good luck selling your house, dear." She waved and walked on down the sidewalk.

Lucy frowned. Maybe that's what everyone thought. That *she* was for sale instead of the *house*.

She dashed inside and grabbed her markers. The sign was fixed in a few minutes. She also gulped down a big glass of water. Trying to sell a house was hot work.

Boo lay down in front of the refrigerator and wouldn't budge.

When Lucy ran back outside, a very interesting sight met her eyes.

7

New Neighbors

A minivan and a car pulled into the driveway of the house next door. The old neighbors had moved out a month ago.

Lucy sat on her grass and held her sign. She watched the commotion next door out of the corners of her eyes. She didn't want to look too nosy. Her mom always said there was nothing worse than a nosy neighbor.

When the cab door of the minivan opened, a dark-haired man climbed out.

Next, one of the car doors opened and out jumped a boy. He looked like he was in first grade, Lucy decided.

Then came the mother. She wore a dress with colorful flowers on it.

Then came the girl.

Lucy couldn't help it. Her heart beat faster and she stared.

The girl looked about her age. She had long black hair in two braids. And she wore a bright dress like her mother's.

"Manuel," the mother called to the little boy. "Stay in our yard."

The father opened the back of the van. It was filled with boxes and furniture.

Slowly and carefully, the mother and father unloaded the van and carried everything inside. The girl helped, too.

The boy just rolled around in the yard. Every once in a while he looked over at Lucy and grinned.

Lucy smiled back.

Finally almost all the furniture and boxes were unloaded. The girl pulled a long rope out of the van. "Can you put up the swing now, Papa?"

Her father put down a big box. "Okay, *niña*," he said. He took the end of the rope and draped it over his shoulder.

Lucy tried not to stare, but she couldn't help it. Her mouth dropped open as the girl's father climbed the tree in the front yard. He tied the rope around a thick branch. Then he slid down the rope. On the end of the rope hung a tire.

"Thank you, Papa," said the girl.

Her father bent down and hugged her. "No problem, *niña*."

The girl climbed onto the swing and twirled around. Her braids flew out from her head like two black snakes.

Finally she stopped twirling. She stared back at Lucy.

Lucy smiled and waved.

The girl waved back.

Forgetting about her FOR SALE sign, Lucy got up and walked to the edge of her lawn.

The girl jumped out of the tire and walked over to Lucy.

"Hi, I'm Lucy," Lucy said.

The girl smiled. "My name is Angelique."

"I thought your dad called you Neenya," Lucy said, confused.

Angelique laughed. "Papa called me *niña*. That means little girl in Spanish."

"Oh," said Lucy, smiling. "My dad calls me pudding pop sometimes. Are you from Spain?"

"No," Angelique said. She pulled on one of her braids. "We're from Mexico. My mother just got a job at a computer company so we moved up here. I've never seen the snow."

Lucy's eyes widened. "Really? We get a lot of it here. I'll teach you how to build a snowman."

"You will?" Angelique clapped her hands together. "I can't wait."

Lucy laughed. "Well, you'll have to wait a long time for that. At least three months."

Just then Angelique's brother hopped over to them on one leg.

"This is Manuel. He's in first grade," Angelique said.

Manuel took his sister's hand, suddenly acting shy.

"Hi, Manuel," said Lucy. "My sister is the same age as you. Her name is Maddy. Maybe you can play with her when she gets home."

Manuel smiled. *"Sí,"* he said.

"Say yes," Angelique said. "No more Spanish now that we're in America."

"It's okay," said Lucy. "There are a lot of people who speak Spanish around here. I even know how to say hello and good-bye."

"Good-bye," Manuel said, scurrying away.

"Adiós," Lucy called after him.

"What grade are you in?" Angelique asked.

"Third. How about you?"

Angelique beamed. "I'm in third too. I have Miss Wengertsman for a teacher."

Lucy squealed. "So do I! She's really cool. We call her Miss W."

The girls laughed and danced in a circle.

Lucy finally stopped, gasping for breath. It was too hot to dance for too long.

Angelique pointed to Lucy's sign, still in the front yard. "What were you doing before?"

Lucy looked at the sign. She had forgotten about selling the house. "Oh, that's nothing," she said quickly. "I have to go throw away that old piece of cardboard. I'll be right back."

8

A New Friend

After throwing away the FOR SALE sign, Lucy ran back outside. "I saw your father climb the tree. He's very fast."

"So am I," Angelique said. "Watch." She hitched up her skirt and climbed the tree as fast as a cat.

"Wow," Lucy said. "I wish I could do that."

Angelique peered down through the branches. "It's easy. I'll teach you."

For the next hour, Angelique taught Lucy how to climb a tree.

"Ow," Lucy said. She brushed off her knees. "Now I have five scratches, two bruises, and a sore elbow. And I still can't climb the tree as fast as you."

Angelique jumped down from the lowest branch. "At least you don't have a broken arm. Yet."

Lucy laughed. "I'm thirsty. Do you want to come over to my house for some lemonade?"

"Let me ask Mama." Angelique ran into her house and came out a minute later. "I can go." She put her arm around Lucy. "I'm glad we moved here. At first I didn't want to come, but now I'm happy."

Lucy put her arm around her new friend. "I'm happy too."

Together, they walked into Lucy's house.

Mrs. Falwell was still working at the kitchen table. She looked up and smiled.

"This is my new friend Angelique," Lucy told her mother. "She's moving in next door."

"How wonderful," said Mrs. Falwell. She got

up and poured them some lemonade. "I'm sure you'll like our town, Angelique."

Angelique smiled. "I already do."

"I'm going to go up and help Mr. Falwell clean the house. See you later, girls."

"Come upstairs and I'll show you my unicorn collection," Lucy said.

In her room, Lucy proudly showed her new friend all her unicorns.

Angelique sighed. "These are beautiful. May I pick one up?"

"Of course," Lucy said. She handed Angelique her biggest and most favorite unicorn of all. It had a gold horn.

Angelique petted the unicorn. "Are there a lot of kids in the neighborhood?"

Lucy shrugged. "I guess so."

"I bet they are all your friends," Angelique said.

Lucy looked at her littlest unicorn. She didn't want to tell Angelique that her friends didn't like her anymore.

So she said, "There are some very nice kids at school. Molly lives down the street. Tasha lives over one block. Pegi lives down the street and around the corner. She has a pool where we go swimming all summer."

"I like to swim," Angelique said. "I used to swim all the time in Mexico."

"Timmy lives nearby," Lucy continued. "He's real funny. And Maryellen and Ricky live on Strawberry Lane. Lesley lives near the school over that way." She pointed toward the living room. "And she owns her very own pony! Judy and Oliver live over on Cranberry Drive."

"Wow," said Angelique. "That's a lot of kids. I wonder if they'll like me."

Lucy sighed softly. "I'm sure they'll like you." They just don't like me anymore, she added silently.

Angelique smiled. "At least I've made one friend so far."

Lucy brightened. "A good friend."

9

Special Buddies

Monday morning, Lucy waited for Angelique outside. Angelique skipped out of her house. "I'm so excited to start a new school now that I have a friend."

Lucy smiled. "We have to hurry so we're not late."

They walked quickly to school.

Along the way, Lucy saw her friends. Only

they weren't her friends anymore, she reminded herself.

They all smiled and waved and stared at Angelique. But when they thought she wasn't looking, Lucy saw them whisper to each other. And they giggled behind their hands.

Lucy lifted her chin. She *wouldn't* let it bother her. She had a new friend now.

In the classroom, Miss W asked Angelique to stand in front of the class.

"Good morning, everyone," she said. She put her hand on Angelique's shoulder. "This is our new student. Angelique comes from Mexico."

Everyone whispered excitedly and clapped.

Angelique blushed.

Lucy smiled at her friend.

"Angelique lives next door to Lucy, therefore I'm going to assign Angelique to this seat." Miss W directed Angelique to the table and chair right next to Lucy. "They will be special buddies for this month."

Lucy thought her heart might burst with happiness. This was the first month of school. She and Angelique would be special buddies until October. And all through the rest of the year too.

NY

Just before reading group, Lesley walked over to Lucy. "What are you doing after school today?"

Lucy looked down at her book. "I'm probably going to play with my new friend."

"Oh," Lesley said. "Are you sure?"

Lucy looked at her. "Pretty sure. Why?"

"Oh, nothing," Lesley said. Her face turned red. "I was just wondering."

Lucy watched Lesley walk back to her desk. Why did she ask me that? Lucy wondered. Maybe—

Miss W interrupted her thoughts. "Open your books to page nine."

Lucy opened her book. The rest of the morning passed quickly.

When the bell rang for recess, Lucy had to finish one more sentence of writing.

"I'll meet you outside," she said to Angelique.

Angelique smiled. "Okay."

Lucy hurried through her assignment. Finally she ran up and placed her paper on Miss W's desk.

"Just a minute, Lucy," Miss W said.

Lucy looked out the window. She didn't see Angelique.

Miss W tapped a piece of chalk on her desk. "It's very nice what you're doing for Angelique."

"She's my friend," Lucy said.

"I know. That's what I mean. You're a good friend to have, Lucy." Miss W smiled. "Go on out to recess now."

Lucy smiled and dashed outside.

Angelique was nowhere to be seen. Where could she be?

There. Lucy caught a glimpse of her bright skirt. She was surrounded by a crowd of kids.

Lucy's heart dropped. They were all talking and laughing.

Lucy slowly walked over to the crowd. Suddenly they stopped what they were doing. They stood silent. Pegi looked at the ground. Oliver shuffled his feet. Maryellen tugged on her cat T-shirt.

Even Angelique looked guilty.

Pegi broke the silence. "Let's play four square." She ran off to the other side of the playground. Molly, Lesley, Judy, and Maryellen raced after her.

"I'm going to play basketball," Timmy said, speeding away with Ricky and Oliver and Pegi close at his heels.

Pretty soon, only Lucy and Angelique were standing there.

"They are all very nice," Angelique said, smiling. "I'm more sure than ever I'm going to like it here."

That makes one of us, Lucy thought.

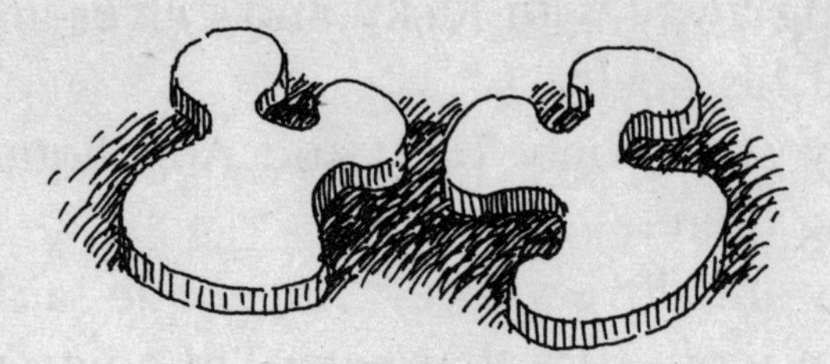

10

Alone Again

After school, Lucy and Angelique left together.

Pegi waved. "Bye you two," she called. "See you later—I mean—"

Ricky jabbed her in the ribs. He dragged her away.

Angelique shrugged, then smiled at Lucy. "Come on, let's go."

Together they walked the one block home.

"Do you want to come over and finish that puzzle we started yesterday?" Lucy asked.

Angelique kicked the sidewalk with the toe of her shoe. "Uh, I can't. I—I have to go to the dentist."

"Do you have a cavity?"

"No, I mean yes. That's right. I have a cavity. A great big one." Angelique lifted her hand to her cheek. "Ouch, it really hurts."

Lucy patted her on the back. "I hope you feel better."

Angelique's cheeks turned red. "Thank you," she said. Then she turned and ran up the walk to her house.

Lucy entered her own house.

"How was school?" her mother asked.

"Good," Lucy said. "Angelique gets to sit next to me and be my special buddy for the rest of the month."

Mrs. Falwell smiled. "That's wonderful."

"She can't come over this afternoon, though. She has to go to the dentist."

Her mother stood up. "That's just as well. I need you to run some errands with me." She checked her watch. "We'll leave in fifteen minutes."

Just then the phone rang. Mrs. Falwell answered it. Maybe it was Angelique. Maybe she didn't have to go to the dentist after all.

"Oh, hi," said her mother.

Lucy sighed. Obviously, it wasn't for her.

Mrs. Falwell quickly took the phone upstairs.

Lucy lugged her book bag into the living room to start her homework.

She'd do her writing first to get it over with. She'd save math, her favorite, for last.

Just as she was opening her notebook, she glanced out the window.

Her heart squeezed tight.

There was Angelique walking down the sidewalk. But she wasn't going to the dentist. Not unless Pegi was going with her. And not unless they gave presents to their dentist.

Lucy slammed her book shut. Half of her wanted to run outside and find out what was going on. The other half of her wanted to run upstairs and cry.

With a heavy sigh, Lucy watched the two girls disappear around the corner.

"Okay, let's go," said her mother cheerily.

"I don't feel like going," Lucy said.

"Come on. I really need your help."

Slowly, Lucy stood up. She may as well go. It wouldn't do any good to sit around and mope. At least that's what her father always told her.

But sometimes moping felt good. Really good.

11

Running Errands

"First I have to go to the grocery store," said Mrs. Falwell.

Lucy stared out the side window. "For what?"

"I have to get, uh, paper plates."

Lucy's eyebrows pulled together. "Paper plates? What for?"

"I have a meeting tomorrow. That's right, I need them for the meeting."

Lucy rolled her eyes. Now her mother was beginning to stammer like her friends. It was as if everyone were making up things to tell her.

They stopped at the store and they both ran in.

"How do you like these?" her mother asked.

Lucy looked at the plates. "*I* like them. But I don't know if your friends will. They're kind of wild plates for old people, aren't they?"

Mrs. Falwell raised her eyebrows. "Old?"

Lucy giggled. "Not you, Mom, just your friends."

"Hmph," said her mother, but she grinned too.

When they got back in the car, Mrs. Falwell said, "Now a quick stop at Mrs. McCarthy's house."

"Oh no," Lucy groaned. "I don't want to go to Lesley's house."

"Why not?"

Lucy looked down at the seat belt buckle.

"Honey," said Mrs. Falwell. "What's the matter?"

"Lesley doesn't like me anymore," Lucy mumbled.

"I'm sure you're wrong," her mother said.

She covered Lucy's hand and squeezed. "You and Lesley are great friends."

"Not anymore. She doesn't like me. No one does."

Mrs. Falwell gasped. "Are you sure?"

Lucy nodded.

"How do you know?"

"On Friday they started whispering about me. They didn't want to do anything with me this weekend. And today, Angelique said she had to go to the dentist. But I saw her walking by with Pegi. I think they were going to a party."

"Why do you think that?" asked her mother.

"They were carrying presents."

"Hmmm. Well, here we are." She pulled up to the curb in front of Lesley's house.

Lucy looked at her mother. She didn't look upset. Maybe she just didn't understand how much she missed her friends.

Mrs. Falwell jumped out of the car. "Come on, Lucy."

Lucy shook her head. "I'm going to stay here."

Her mother stuck her head in the window. "I need your help carrying something. Come on."

Lucy clenched her teeth and climbed out of

the car. Hopefully Lesley wouldn't be home. She's probably at the party I wasn't invited to, Lucy thought.

She walked up the front path as slowly as possible.

Her mother nudged her from behind. "You're as slow as a snail today. Hurry up."

Finally Lucy reached the front door. She reached for the buzzer, when suddenly the door burst open.

12

Surprise!

"SURPRISE!" everyone yelled.

Lucy's mouth dropped open.

Crowding in the door stood all her classmates. Even Angelique was there.

"What?" Lucy squeaked.

"SURPRISE!" they all shouted again.

"Surprise?" Lucy repeated.

Her mother squeezed her shoulders. "Are you surprised, Lucy?"

Lesley stepped forward. "This is a surprise party for you."

Lucy couldn't shut her mouth. "For me? But it's not even my birthday."

Lesley hugged her. "We know. We're having a party for you because you're such a good friend."

"A—a friend?" Lucy stammered. Now she was doing it!

"A really good friend," Timmy said, grinning. "You always laugh at my jokes."

"Even the crummy ones," Oliver added with a grin.

"But I thought none of you liked me," Lucy said.

"What?" Tasha exclaimed. "Why did you think that?"

"Because you all were talking about me."

"We were planning your party!" Judy said.

Lucy laughed. "I thought you were telling secrets about me. And laughing!"

"We weren't laughing at you," Pegi said. "We were laughing about how surprised you'd be."

Ricky pulled Lucy into the house. "Come in. See what we've done."

Everyone followed Lucy into the living room.

Lucy gasped. The whole room was decorated with rainbows and unicorns.

"We know you love rainbows and unicorns so much, so that's our theme for your party," Oliver explained. "What do you think?"

"It took us all weekend to cut out those rainbows," Maryellen added.

"I love it," Lucy said. "And that explains why no one could do anything with me this weekend."

Molly pointed to the decorations. "We were very busy."

Lucy laughed. "I guess so." She turned to Angelique. "You didn't have to go to the dentist, did you?"

Angelique blushed. "I didn't want to lie to you, but your friends invited me to your surprise party."

Lucy hugged her. "That's okay. I'm just so glad I *have* friends!"

"Time for the presents," Lesley announced.

"Yeah." Everyone cheered.

"Presents for me?" Lucy said, her eyes wide.

Maryellen handed her a small package. "We can't have a party without presents."

Lucy unwrapped the package. It was a bookmark.

"I made it myself," Maryellen said proudly.

"Thank you so much," Lucy said.

Next she unwrapped a gift Molly handed her. "A chocolate unicorn!" Lucy exclaimed, her eyes wide with pleasure.

Molly beamed. "I made it myself using a mold. When I saw the unicorn mold, I knew it was perfect for you."

"Thank you, thank you," Lucy said, carefully putting the chocolate unicorn to the side. She continued opening gifts.

Each present was wonderful. And each present was homemade, which made it even better.

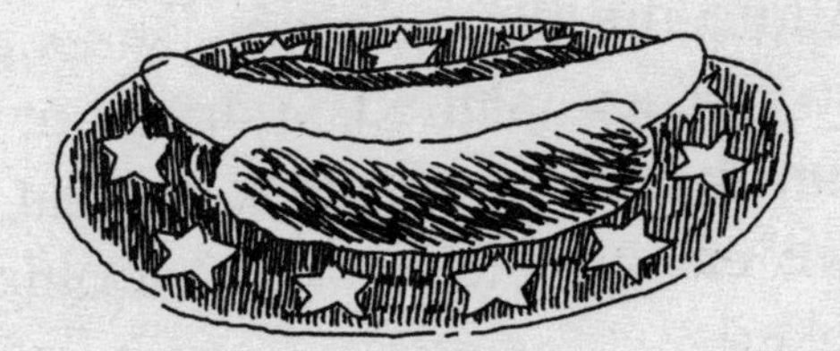

13

Rid of the Blues and Out of the Dumps

After the presents, Jamal said, "Isn't it time to eat yet?"

Tasha laughed. "All you think about is food," she teased.

Jamal grinned. "So?"

Ricky stood next to his friend and put his arm across Jamal's shoulders. "I'm hungry too."

Pegi stepped forward. "Me too!"

"Then we better eat," Lesley said. She led everyone into the dining room.

"Ooooo." Lucy sighed, staring at all the goodies on the table. "Look at all that food."

"Can we eat it instead of just looking at it?" Timmy joked.

"Lucy gets to go first," Sue announced. "She's the guest of honor." She handed Lucy a paper plate.

"Hey," Lucy said, "these plates look familiar."

Her mother laughed. "Mrs. McCarthy called me right before we left. She had forgotten to get them. So you got to pick out your own pattern."

Lucy looked at the food and hesitated. Everything looked so good, she didn't know where to start.

"Hurry up," urged Jamal right behind her. "Just take one of everything like I always do."

Lucy took his suggestion. Everything looked too tasty to pass up. By the time she'd walked around the whole table, her plate was overflowing.

Chairs were set up in the living room for people to sit on. And there were also large pillows

on the floor. They were from Lesly's bedroom. Lucy chose a bright pink pillow to sit on.

Pretty soon all her friends joined her.

Maryellen picked up something off her plate. She scrunched her nose.

"What's this?"

"Those are banana dogs," Sue said.

"Banana dogs?" Maryellen squeaked.

"Jutht try it," Jamal said with his mouth full. "Ith deliciouth."

Maryellen took a small bite and chewed. Everyone watched her. After she swallowed, a big smile spread across her face. "Yummy!"

Everyone laughed and took big bites out of their own banana dogs.

Lucy couldn't stop laughing and smiling. She looked around at all her friends. Her real, true friends.

A surprise party, she decided, was the best way to get rid of the blues and out of the dumps.

PARTY PLANNING TIPS:

HOW TO HAVE A SURPRISE PARTY

It's just as much fun to plan a SURPRISE PARTY as it is to be the guest of honor. You can give a surprise party for a friend for any reason. It doesn't have to be for a birthday. In fact, if you plan a party when it's least expected, your friend will be super surprised, just like Lucy was!

Just be sure you don't act strangely in front of the friend who is getting the surprise party. Like Lucy, your friend might wonder why you're whispering and giggling behind her or his back. And the last thing you want to do is hurt your friend's feelings.

Lucy loves unicorns and rainbows, so her friends chose them as the THEME for her surprise party. When you pick a theme for your party, it will help you plan the food, the decorations, and the games. The best way to choose a theme is to pick something the guest of honor will like. Maybe your friend likes dinosaurs or horses, or has a favorite book or movie. Knowing your friend's favorite color will also help you plan the party.

Since this is a surprise party, it's a good idea to make a surprise INVITATION. Just take a piece of paper and fold it in half once, and then once again. Then cut along the inside center fold.

On the front cover of the invitation write SHHHHHHH! Open the invitation, and on the left side write IT'S A SECRET! On the right side write IT'S A SURPRISE! Then on the bottom of the right side write LIFT THE FLAP. Under the flap write

IT'S A SECRET SURPRISE PARTY FOR ______________! Then write all the details for your party.

This clever invitation will get your friends psyched for the big surprise.

At Lucy's surprise party, she and her friends played lots of GAMES. You can take a traditional game and fit it to your party theme. For example, if the theme is dinosaurs, you can play pin the tail on the T-Rex. Lucy and her friends played pin the tail on the . . . unicorn, of course!

Surprise Snacks

Lucy and her friends love to eat, so they had a lot of fun food at her party. They each drank a SURPRISE SODA. Your friends will love them, too! They're a surprise because you can vary the ingredients and they still taste good. Buy a variety of flavored sodas, like cola, root beer, and orange, and a couple of kinds of ice cream, such as vanilla and chocolate. Fill a glass half-way with soda, then plop in a scoop of ice cream. Let your guests mix and match their own flavors. You can also jazz up this drink with a fancy straw.

Here's how to make FANCY STRAWS: First buy regular straws. Next, cut round shapes out of colored construction paper. The circles should be about the size of a half dollar. Then cut two small slits in each circle and slide the straws through. Now you have fancy straws.

You can even decorate the cut-out shapes with glitter, confetti, or other colorful things for extra extra, fancy straws!

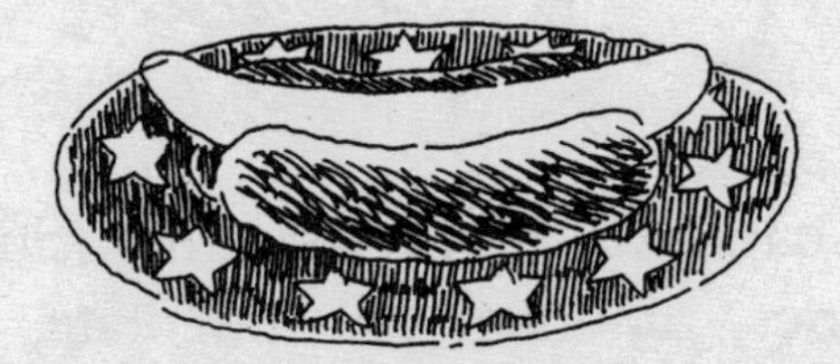

Lesley planned the menu for Lucy's surprise party. She fed her guests BANANA DOGS and everyone loved them. All you have to do is make sure you have enough bananas and hot-dog rolls for each of your friends. Spread each roll with peanut butter on one side and marsh-mallow fluff on the other. Put the banana in the middle, just like you would a hot dog. Finally, spread a little jelly on the banana. And chow down!

For dessert, Lesley served SURPRISE CUP-CAKES. There's a surprise hidden in every one, and they're very easy to make. First, prepare your favorite cupcake batter by following the directions on a box or family recipe. Line a muffin pan with twelve cupcake holders. Pour the batter evenly into the cupcake holders, filling them only half full. Next, put one surprise

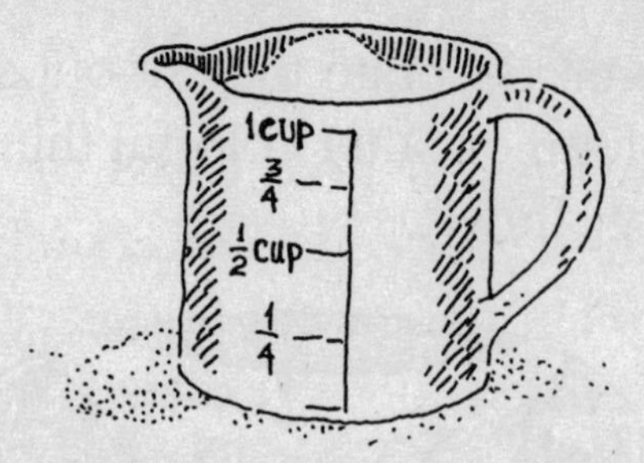

in each cupcake. Surprises can include fresh strawberries, chunks of chocolate, candied nuts, or anything else you think your friends would love. Then cover the surprises with more batter, filling each cupcake ¾ full. Bake your cupcakes in a preheated oven for the time instructed by the recipe. Once they're cool, eat and enjoy the surprise!

Surprise Gifts

Lucy's friends made her a SURPRISE GIFT. You can ask your friends to do this for the guest of honor too. Don't make anything big and expensive. Make something your guest of honor will like. Here are three ideas for nifty surprise gifts.

Note Cards

To make special note cards for your friend to send to her friends and family, take five pieces of plain paper and fold each one in half once, and then once again. These will be your cards.

Find five 4⅜-by-5½-inch envelopes.

Decorate the cards and envelopes with stickers, stamps, glitter, and original drawings. Be sure to leave room inside the cards for your friend to write a sweet or funny message. Leave the fronts of the envelopes clear for the address and stamps.

Tie them all together with a pretty ribbon or yarn.

Bookmark

Take a piece of stiff paper and cut it into a unique and interesting shape. Keep the shape approximately six inches long and two inches wide.

Now decorate it. A nice touch is writing your friend's name on the bookmark. And to make it extra special, punch a hole in the top of the

bookmark and then tie some colorful yarn through it.

Picture Frame

Cut two pieces of cardboard the same size and shape. They should be large enough to be a picture frame.

Take one piece and cut a large shape out of the center, maybe a squiggly square or a heart. Place the center piece that you just cut out aside for later.

Spraypaint one side of each of the large cardboard pieces and let them dry. Make sure you paint the two sides that will form the outsides of the frame.

Glue the two pieces together on three

sides—the two sides and the bottom of what will be your picture frame. Keep the top side unglued so you can slip a photograph or picture into the frame.

Now your frame is ready for decorating. You can glue on pasta, colored beans, or small plastic toys. Or use glitter pens to create a design.

Finally, using the small piece you cut out and put aside, cut out a triangle shape to use for a back stand that will prop the frame up. Fold the triangle in half. Then glue the back of the triangle to the back of the frame to make a stand so the frame can stand up by itself.

Have fun planning your surprise party. Just imagine how surprised your friend will be when she or he opens the door and you all shout "SURPRISE!"